HELLO KITTY®

A Surprise for Mama

ABRADALE

New York

Hello Kitty and Mimmy were very excited. Today, they were going to make Mama something special. What would be a good surprise?

Hello Kitty wanted to make cookies! Mimmy thought this was a wonderful idea. What kind should they make?

Hello Kitty remembered that sugar cookies were Mama's favorite, so she found a cookbook with a sugar cookie recipe.

Hello Kitty got out the flour and salt.
Mimmy got out the sugar.

They also needed eggs, butter, and vanilla. Hello Kitty went to the fridge and took out the ingredients.

Mimmy measured the sugar and flour.
Hello Kitty reminded her not to use
too much flour.

Oh, no! Flour can be very messy!

Eggs can be very messy, too!

Baking cookies looked so easy when Mama did it. How would they ever finish?

Just then, Mama came into the kitchen. Mama knew the girls must be making something special, and she offered to help. The girls were happy Mama was there to help!

While the cookies were baking, everyone cleaned up. Cleaning up is much more fun together!

Even though they were having so much fun, Hello Kitty was a little sad. After all, the cookies were supposed to be a surprise, but the girls had needed Mama's help to make them.

But Hello Kitty felt better when Mama
hugged her. Baking with Mama was the
best surprise ever!

They took the cookies and glasses of milk
into the garden. It was time to try the cookies!
They all agreed, they were delicious!

ISBN 978-1-4197-0650-9

Text, illustrations, and original art copyright © SANRIO CO., LTD.

© 1976, 2013 SANRIO CO., LTD. Used Under License. www.sanrio.com

Published in 2013 by Abradale, an imprint of Abrams. All rights reserved.
No portion of this book may be reproduced, stored in a retrieval system,
or transmitted in any form or by any means, mechanical, electronic, photocopying,
recording, or otherwise, without written permission from the publisher.

Printed and bound in China
10 9 8 7 6 5 4 3 2

THE ART OF BOOKS SINCE 1949
115 West 18th Street
New York, NY 10011
www.abramsbooks.com